For Nicole and Jason —
love will keep you safe from the storm

Bloomsbury Publishing, London, New Delhi, New York and Sydney

First published in the United States of America in 2015
by Bloomsbury Children's Books
1385 Broadway, New York, New York 10018

This edition first published in Great Britain in 2015 by Bloomsbury Publishing Plc
50 Bedford Square, London, WC1B 3DP

A CIP catalogue record of this book is available from the British Library

ISBN 978 1 4088 6231 5

Printed in China by Leo Paper Products, Heshan, Guangdong

1 3 5 7 9 10 8 6 4 2

www.bloomsbury.com

# STORMY NIGHT

## Salina Yoon

BLOOMSBURY

LONDON  NEW DELHI  NEW YORK  SYDNEY

One stormy night,
Bear couldn't sleep.

The wind was whirring, the trees were crackling and the rain was pounding against the windows.

"Don't worry," said Bear.
"I'll hold you tight. I'll keep you warm.
My love will keep you safe from the storm,"

he sang to his bunny, Floppy.

Bear felt better.

But when a thundering sound rumbled through the forest, it startled Bear.

He sang his song again.

Mama came in to check on Bear.
"May I stay with you tonight? I am
so frightened by the storm!"

Bear was glad to see Mama.

He kissed Mama's nose to comfort her. Mama smiled.

Bear felt better.

Then Papa came in to check
on Bear. "Is there room for me?
The storm is so loud tonight!"

Bear was glad to see Papa.
He tickled Papa's ear to comfort him.

Papa laughed! And Bear felt better.

"But what will make Floppy feel better?" thought Bear. "I know!"

"A book!"

"This is a bear-y good book!"

Bear almost forgot about the storm until . . .

# OM!

A loud, crashing sound of thunder roared through the forest.

Bear shut his eyes tight.

Mama kissed his nose,

and Papa tickled his ear.

Mama sang to Bear just like
she did when he was a little cub.

"We'll hold you tight. We'll keep you warm.
Our love will keep you safe from the storm."
Bear felt better.

Bear yawned a sleepy yawn, and then it was quiet. "What happened to the storm?"

"Even storms need their sleep!" said Papa.

And so do bears!